With special thanks to dinosaur specialist and paleontologist, Dr. Matthew Lamanna, for his review and advice on the writing of this book.
—D. P.

Parent's Introduction

We Both Read is the first series of books designed to invite parents and children to share the reading of a story by taking turns reading aloud. This "shared reading" innovation, which was developed with reading education specialists, invites parents to read the more complex text and storyline on the left-hand pages. Children are encouraged to read the right-hand pages, which feature less complex text and storyline, specifically written for the beginning reader.

Reading aloud is one of the most important activities parents can share with their child to assist them in their reading development. However, *We Both Read* goes beyond reading **to** a child and allows parents to share the reading **with** a child. *We Both Read* is so powerful and effective because it combines two key elements in learning: "modeling" (the parent reads) and "doing" (the child reads). The result is not only faster reading development for the child, but a much more enjoyable and enriching experience for both!

You may find it helpful to read the entire book aloud yourself the first time, then invite your child to participate in the second reading. In some books, a few more difficult words will first be introduced in the parent's text, distinguished with **bold lettering**. Pointing out, and even discussing, these words will help familiarize your child with them and help to build your child's vocabulary. Also, note that a "talking parent" icon ☺ precedes the parent's text and a "talking child" icon ☺ precedes the child's text.

We encourage you to share and interact with your child as you read the book together. If your child is having difficulty, you might want to mention a few things to help them. "Sounding out" is good, but it will not work with all words. Children can pick up clues about the words they are reading from the story, the context of the sentence, or even the pictures. Some stories have rhyming patterns that might help. It might also help them to touch the words with their finger as they read, to better connect the voice sound and the printed word.

Sharing the *We Both Read* books together will engage you and your child in an interactive adventure in reading! It is a fun and easy way to encourage and help your child to read—and a wonderful way to start them off on a lifetime of reading enjoyment!

We Both Read: About Dinosaurs

—————————————————————

We Both Read® is a registered trademark of Treasure Bay, Inc.

Published by Treasure Bay, Inc.
17 Parkgrove Drive
South San Francisco, CA 94080 USA

PRINTED IN SINGAPORE

Library of Congress Catalog Card Number: 2003115521

Hardcover ISBN: 1-891327-53-4
Paperback ISBN: 1-891327-54-2

FIRST EDITION

We Both Read® Books
Patent No. 5,957,693

Visit us online at:
www.webothread.com

About Dinosaurs

By Sindy McKay
Illustrated by Robert Walters

TREASURE BAY

Millions of years ago, animals we call **dinosaurs** lived all over the world. These **dinosaurs** are now *extinct,* but you can still see them in movies, books, and even in museums.

In Greek, the word "**dinosaur**" means "terrible **lizard.**" But in fact, **dinosaurs** were neither terrible nor lizards.

Chameleon—a lizard

Gargoyleosaurus (gar-GOYL-e-o-SAWR-us)— a dinosaur

Lizards stand with their legs to the side of their bodies. Dinosaurs stood with their legs under their bodies.

Paleontologist with duck-billed dinosaur jaw

   The scientists who study dinosaurs are called *paleontologists (PAY-lee-on-TOL-a-jists).*

By studying fossil bones, paleontologists have identified over 300 different kinds of dinosaurs. But most believe that there may be at least twice that many dinosaurs that have not yet been discovered.

Bones of this dinosaur were discovered just a few years ago. It lived 110 million years ago.

Paleontologists agree that dinosaurs were reptiles. They lived on land, breathed air, and did not fly. Like modern birds, dinosaurs hatched from eggs.

The largest dinosaur eggs that have been found are about the size of a football. That's a lot bigger than a chicken egg!

Some dinosaurs walked on two legs. Some walked on four legs. Some could do both.

Carnivores–Tyrannosaurus rex (tie-RAN-oh-SORE-us rex) and Dromaeosaurus (DROH-may-oh-SORE-us) Herbivores–Styracosaurus (Stie-rak-a-SORE-us) and Alamosaurus (Al-a-mo-SORE-us)

Dinosaurs like Tyrannosaurus rex (tie-RAN-oh-SORE-us rex) and Dromaeosaurus (DROH-may-oh-SORE-us) ate only meat. They were *carnivores.*

Most carnivores are **predators.** That means they hunt other animals, called *prey.* Some carnivores are *scavengers.* That means they eat meat that they did not kill themselves.

Tarbosaurus (TAHR-bo-SORE-us) and Therizinosaurus (Ther-i-Zin-oh-SORE-us)

Being a **predator** was not easy. You often had to fight sharp horns and long claws. If you were hurt and could not hunt, you would die.

Stegosaurus (Steg-o-SORE-us) and Ceratosaurus (Ser-a-to-SORE-us)

Stegosaurus (Steg-o-SORE-us) was just one of the many dinosaurs that were *herbivores*. They ate only plants.

Some herbivores also swallowed rocks, called gastroliths (GAS-troe-liths), to help grind up the fibers of tough plants in their guts.

A few dinosaurs may have been **omnivores**.

Prenocephale (pren-oh-SEF-a-lee) dinosaurs butting heads

 Being an **omnivore** means that you eat both meat and plants. This kind of dinosaur might have eaten bugs, small animals, eggs, seeds, and leaves.

Some people think all dinosaurs were huge. And many of them WERE! Brachiosaurus (BRACK-ee-uh-SORE-us) was taller than a four-story building. The neck of a Sauroposeidon (SORE-oh-po-SIE-don) was longer than a school bus. But as huge as these animals were, none were as big as the blue whale that lives in our oceans today.

Compsognathus (komp-soh-NAY-thus)

This dinosaur was very small. It was about as big as a chicken. It could run very fast. It ate bugs and lizards.

Camarasaurus (KAM-a-rah-SORE-us) dinosaurs (about 60 feet long)
being pursued by Allosaurus (al-uh-SORE-us) dinosaurs

Despite their ferocious reputation, most dinosaurs were herbivores that traveled in herds with their family. Tracks indicate that the youngest members traveled in the middle of the herd for the most protection from predators.

There may have been hundreds, even thousands of members in one herd.

   This plant-eating dinosaur would nip off plants with its sharp beak. Then, it used its teeth to grind up the plants.

Massospondylus (mas-o-SPON-di-lus) and pack of Megapnosaurus (Meg-ap-no-SORE-us)

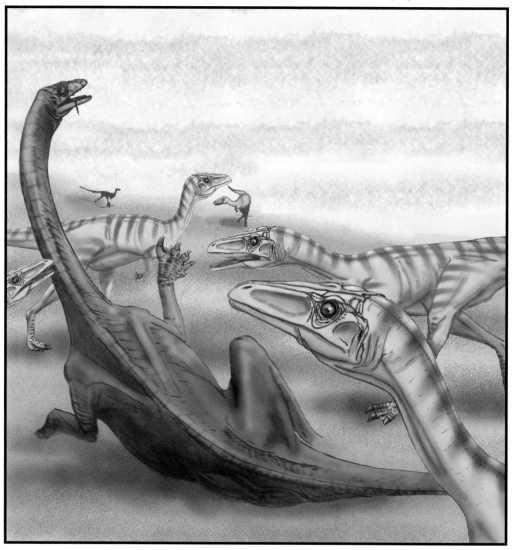

Herbivores were probably not the only dinosaurs that lived in groups. Some carnivores may have also gathered in packs. In this way, smaller predators could cooperate in hunting large prey, similar to modern day **wolves**.

Daspletosaurus (das-PLEET-oh-SORE-us)

These two dinosaurs were much bigger than **wolves**. But some people think that they may have hunted in packs, too.

Many plant-eating dinosaurs had built-in weapons to protect them from meat-eating predators. Triceratops (tri-SER-a-tops) had three sharp horns and probably charged into its enemy the same way a modern rhinoceros does.

Ankylosaurus (an-KIE-loh-SORE-us)

Some dinosaurs had bony plates on their bodies. Even big, sharp teeth may not have been able to bite through them.

Huge dinosaurs like Rebbachisaurus (re-BAK-i-SORE-us), which could be up to 60 feet long, didn't worry too much about **predators**. But being big didn't always mean you were safe.

Some **predators** did hunt the giant dinosaurs.
A giant dinosaur was a lot to eat, even for a pack
of hungry predators.

Altirhinus (al-ti-RINE-us)

No one knows for sure the color of any dinosaur. But by figuring out how a dinosaur lived, scientists can look at modern animals that live in a similar manner and make educated guesses. For example, unprotected herbivores may have had skin colors that helped to camouflage them.

Caudipteryx (caw-DIP-ter-iks)

Some dinosaurs were covered in feathers. These feathers were not used for flying. They probably helped to keep the animal warm.

MAMENCHISAURUS (mah-MEN-chee-SORE-us) (neck length up to 33 feet)

Paleontologists can determine how fast or slow a dinosaur moved by examining the footprints some dinosaurs left behind.

It's not surprising to learn that the slowest dinosaurs were the huge herbivores like Mamenchisaurus (mah-MEN-chee-SORE-us).

These dinosaurs didn't need to be in a hurry. Besides having long necks and long tails, they had long lives. Some lived to be 80 years old!

Ingenia (in-GAY-nee-a)

The fastest dinosaurs were probably the small carnivores like this Ingenia (in-GAY-nee-a). These dinosaurs ran on two legs and used their tail to help with balance so they could change direction quickly as they ran.

Ornitholestes (OR-nith-OH-LES-teez) being chased by Allosaurus (al-oh-SORE-us)

Running fast was important to small dinosaurs. It helped them to catch their **prey**. And it helped to keep them from BECOMING prey!

Most of us know that humans were not around during the time of the dinosaurs. But sometimes movies and books put other mammals and **reptiles** with the dinosaurs that were not there either.

This mammoth, which is now **extinct**, lived about 60 million years after the dinosaurs.

 This large **reptile** may look like a dinosaur. But it became **extinct** about 40 million years BEFORE the first dinosaur was born!

Not all dinosaurs lived at the same time either. Different kinds of dinosaurs lived at different times.

The Centrosaurus (SEN-troh-SORE-us) on this page lived about 70 million years after the Torvosaurus (TORE-voe-SORE-us) on the next page.

Torvosaurus (TORE-voe-SORE-us)

Dinosaurs were on the earth for a very long time. They lasted about 160 million years.

So what happened to all these great dinosaurs? No one is absolutely sure, but most scientists believe there was a major change in the environment when an asteroid hit the Earth. The sun's light was blocked, causing plants to die and depleting the dinosaurs' source of food and water.

Protoarchaeopteryx (Pro-tar-kee-OP-ter-iks)

Many people think there aren't any dinosaurs left on earth. But that may not be true.

Scientists now believe that modern birds may be descendants of dinosaurs.

This Archaeopteryx (ar-kee-OP-ter-iks) is the creature that started it all. When its fossils were found, biologists noted the similarities between this ancient bird and meat-eating dinosaurs.

Whistling swan

Next time you see a bird in the sky, remember —you may be looking at a modern dinosaur!

Jawbone of dinosaur

One way to learn about dinosaurs is by studying *fossils.* Fossils are remains of dead animals and plants preserved in rocks. The fossil of a bone isn't really a bone at all. It has the same shape as the bone, but it is really more like a rock.

Fossils of these two mighty dinosaurs were found buried together. They must have fought each other to the death.

A full skeleton of Tarbosaurus (TAHR-bo-SORE-us) on display at a museum.

 People have been finding dinosaur fossils for hundreds, maybe thousands of years. But no one knew what they were or what to call the animals until Sir Richard Owen coined the name "dinosaur" in 1842.

Many museums have dinosaur fossils on display. Visiting one of these museums is a great way to see dinosaurs up close.

 Clues about dinosaurs have been found all over the world. Who knows? Maybe someday you will discover a dinosaur right in your own backyard!

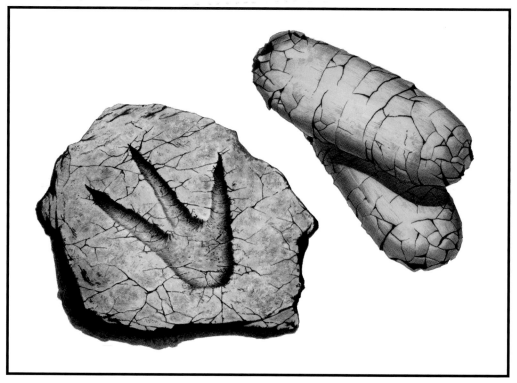

OTHER WORDS TO KNOW

Extinct – no longer in existence

Paleontologist – a scientist who studies dinosaurs

Carnivore – an animal that eats meat

Herbivore – an animal that eats plants

Omnivore – an animal that eats both meat and plants

Predator – an animal that hunts other animals for food

Prey – an animal that is hunted for food

Scavenger – an animal that eats meat that it does not kill itself

Fossil – preserved remains or imprint of a living thing

NAME ROOTS

What do the names mean?

Acro – high

Archaeo – ancient

Brachy - short

Carno – flesh

Centro – left

Cephalo- head

Cera – horn

Compso – elegant

Coryth – helmet

Dino – fearfully great or terrible

Dromeo - runner

Giga – savage giant

Hadro – large

Lestes – robber

Krito – chosen or separated

Mimus - mimic

Plateo – flat

Preno – sloping

Proto – first or earliest

Pteryx – wing or fin

Raptor – plunderer

Rhinus – nose or snout

Saurus – lizard

Stego – roof or cover

Suchus - crocodile

Tri – three

Tyranno – tyrant

Veloci – speedy

If you liked
***About Dinosaurs*, here are two other**
We Both Read ® **Books you are sure to enjoy!**

Over 20 different kinds of insects are featured in this non-fiction book in the *We Both Read*™ series. With 40 pages of amazing photographs of the insect world, this book relates fascinating facts about these six-legged creatures that will enthrall children and parents alike!